The BUTTERFLY DANCE

TO JOHN

The
BUTTERFLY DANCE

Story and Illustrations by
Gerald Dawavendewa

Tales of the People

National Museum of the American Indian,
Smithsonian Institution
Washington, D.C., and New York

Abbeville Press Publishers
New York   London

Today is a special day. I wake up extra early because this is the day of the Butterfly Dance.

My name is Sihumana, which means Flower Maiden. My aunt gave me that name in a special naming ceremony when I was just a baby. Now I am twelve years old, and today I will be a part of the Butterfly Dance, helping to celebrate our family and bring gentle rains for the flowers and plants that will make everyone happy.

First I go with Kwa'a, my grandfather, to greet the sun. Kwa'a knows about our people and the world around us, and he teaches me more every day.

Kwa'a blesses the day with sacred cornmeal, which he carefully sprinkles in the wind to carry our prayers. "It is good to be here this morning," he says, "for today is a special day. Sihumana is going to dance in the Butterfly Dance!"

7

After Kwa'a and I come back home, it is time to eat breakfast. I am too excited to eat much, even though we have my favorites—bean-sprout soup with the flat bread we call *piiki*.

"Eat, Sihumana!" says So'o, my grandmother. "You will need food to dance." We all sit down on the floor to eat, though my baby sister, Siwa, sleeps through breakfast.

After breakfast, it is time for my family to go with me to the village where the Butterfly Dance is held at the end of every summer.

Before I leave, my best friend, Sakwapumana, gives me sweet blue-corn snacks. "Just like your name, Sakwapumana!" I say, because Sakwapumana means Blue Corn Maiden.

"Have a good trip, Sihumana," says Sakwapumana. "My family will not leave till later, but I will see you at the dance. We would not miss this special day!"

I say good-bye, and we start on our journey, which will take several hours.

As we walk to the village, Kwa'a tells me why we have the Butterfly Dance.

"When you dance, you celebrate our family and you celebrate the clouds that bring gentle rains. When you dance, Sihumana, you are like a butterfly that flies from flower to flower, helping them grow. You bring rain for the flowers and plants, and you make everyone happy."

I tell Kwa'a it will be fun to be a butterfly!

We arrive at the village, where I find my friend Holetsi, who will be my partner in the Butterfly Dance. We are excited to see each other, for we have spent many days practicing together to prepare for this day.

There are more than thirty Hopi clans. Each Hopi person becomes a part of his or her mother's clan. I am of the Rabbit Clan, and Holetsi is of the Bear Clan. We are partners in the dance because Holetsi's father is of my clan.

Holetsi, whose name means "row of arrows," gives me a headdress that he and his father have made just for me. It is a present for me to keep, and I can't wait to wear it in the dance.

My mother helps me dress for the dance in special clothes, jewelry, and my new headdress. "Your headdress is so pretty," she says. "It is shaped like a cloud, and the designs on it show the flowers that grow with the rain."

I am very nervous about the dance, but my mother tells me not to worry. "You have worked very hard for this, and we are proud of you. We will all be there to watch you."

I wait with the other dancers as we watch the singers and the drummer march into the plaza, an open place in the village where we have our dances. Kwa'a and my father are with the singers, and they are all singing the Butterfly song:

Hapi me Hapi me'e	Verily, listen,
Hapi me Hapi me'e	Verily, listen,
Ayooya	From over there—
Yooyang Anyog'oo	Rain clouds,
	From over there—
Uma'mii Pew'ii	Coming to you here
Ayooya Oongaq	From up above.
Yooyang Anyog'oo	Rain clouds
	From over there—
Uma'mii Pew'ii	Coming to you here.

We dance all afternoon, singing and praying for the rain and for all our families and friends who have come to watch us. We dance to bring the rain to our fields so that we can grow our corn. We dance like butterflies going from flower to flower. I also remember to dance for the bean sprouts that go into my favorite soup.

As we dance, members of many different clans from the village watch us from their houses. And some visitors from other villages watch the Butterfly Dance from the rooftops.

21

When the dance is over, I am tired, but I help my mother take care of my little sister. I take Siwa to sit on the roof with Sakwapumana, and we all look for rain clouds.

"My parents say that next year I can take part in the Butterfly Dance," Sakwapumana says.

"Yes, we can both dance together," I tell her. Sakwapumana thinks that will be fun.

A little while later, we hear a rumble of thunder.

We spend the night at my aunt's house, sleeping in blankets on the floor. Before I sleep, I place my headdress against the wall.

My mother tucks me in and says, "The whole family is proud of you, Sihumana, and I am happy that you took part in the Butterfly Dance, just as your grandmother and I once did."

"I liked dancing to help our family and to make the plants grow and bring the butterflies that come when the clouds give us rain," I tell her.

Just before I fall asleep, I can hear the rain softly falling on the roof, and tomorrow I know I will see beautiful butterflies!

The Butterfly Dance

The Butterfly Dance is one of many dances of the Hopi people. Although primarily social, the Butterfly Dance also has spiritual and religious significance. Its songs are prayers for rain and a happy life. The gathering of the dancers, singers, and other village participants provides the opportunity for communal prayer through song.

The dance, which takes place in late summer and usually lasts two days, is performed by young and unmarried women of the village, whose partners are their *mööyi* (paternal-clan nephews). On the day of the Butterfly Dance, each girl is presented with an elaborate dance headdress, made especially for her by her partner. This headdress of brightly painted wood is a gift kept by the girl after the dance. Each young woman and many of her female-clan relatives give bread and pastries to her dance partner. The male partner reciprocates with gifts of *sikwi* (meat).

Before the dancing begins, male singers and a drummer enter the dance area singing, while the dancers wait and watch. The dancers then take their places in two lines, dancing with their partners in unison to the music. The carefully choreographed dances are rehearsed for several nights in the *kivas* (underground ceremonial chambers). Sometimes new songs, which both the singers and the dancers must learn, are created for the Butterfly Dance.

Hopi Pahlikmana (butterfly) katsina tihu (doll). Oraibi, Arizona. Height: 15 in. (37.5 cm). 9.990

Hopi Ho-o-te katsina by Earl Yowytewa (Hopi, b. 1942). Arizona. Watercolor on paper, 18 x 14 in. (45 x 35 cm). 24.3902

Hopi Hahai katsina tihu (doll), early 20th century. Arizona. Cottonwood root, paint, and feather, height: 7⅝ in. (19 cm). 18.895

Glossary

wicker basket	*yungyapu* (yoong YA poo)
butterfly	*poli* (BO li)
clan	*wungwa* (WOONG wah)
dance	*tiikive* (DEE kee veh)
dress	*manta* (MAHN ta)
Flower Maiden	Sihumana
headdress	*kopatsoki* (koe PAT zo kee)
rain	*yooyang* (Yoo YUNG)
sun	*taawa* (DA wa)
village	*kitsoki* (kit SO kee)
blue-corn flat bread	*piiki* (PEE kee)

Hopi girls. Arizona. N41448

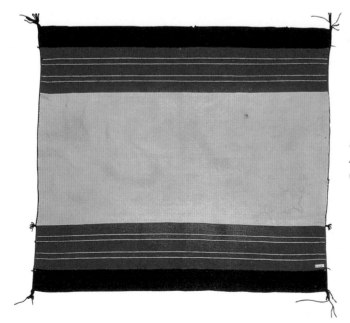

*Hopi woman's cape.
Arizona. 45¼ x 39⅝ in.
(113.1 x 99 cm).* 23.2871

27

The Hopi

For thousands of years the Hopi have lived in villages located on the mesa tops of northern Arizona. One of the Pueblo culture groups of the southwestern United States, the Hopi are descendants of the Hitsatsinom ("people of long ago," sometimes called Anasazi), whose village ruins now dot the Southwest. Today there are approximately 12,000 Hopi individuals, 80 percent of whom live on the Hopi reservation in northern Arizona.

Clan membership, which is traced through the mother, defines certain responsibilities and relationships (including marriage) in Hopi religion and society. Throughout their lives, clan members learn about the specific religious and cultural histories of their clans, as well as the interrelationships between their clan and others within the complex network of Hopi life.

Hopis are predominantly farmers, known especially for growing blue corn in the dry desert, which receives an average of just ten to twelve inches of rain a year. They also grow beans, melons, and peaches. The Hopi believe that by living a good life and by offering songs and prayers for rain, they can help ensure life for their crops and for all people.

Nampeyo (Hopi-Tewa, 1860?-1942), c. 1920-25. Hano, First Mesa, Arizona. P7128

Above left: *Hopi wicker basket with Nuvak (snow katsina) design. Arizona. 15 x 15¼ in. (37.5 x 38 cm).* 23.3760

Left: *Sikyatki-style pot by Nampeyo (Hopi-Tewa, 1860?-1942). Arizona. Painted clay, 13³/₈ x 6³/₄ in. (33.6 x 17.2 cm).* 18.7533

Above: *The Hopi village of Walpi, First Mesa, Arizona.* P10713

Above right: *Niman ceremony, 1919. Walpi, First Mesa, Arizona. The children are holding katsina dolls just given to them by the katsinas.* N27794

Far left: *Hopi man weaving, 1879. Walpi, First Mesa, Arizona.* P3451

Left: *Trail leading to the Hopi village of Walpi, First Mesa, Arizona.* P3538

For Deborah and Karin

Project Director and Head of Publications, NMAI:
  Terence Winch
Photo and Research Editor, NMAI: Lou Stancari
Editor, NMAI: Cheryl Wilson
Content Advisor, NMAI: Susan Secakuku (Hopi)
Executive Editor, Abbeville: Nancy Grubb
Designer, Abbeville: Molly Shields
Production Editor, Abbeville: Kerrie Baldwin
Production Manager, Abbeville: Louise Kurtz

For information about the National Museum of the American Indian, visit the NMAI Website at www.si.edu/nmai.

The National Museum of the American Indian, Smithsonian Institution, is dedicated to working in collaboration with the indigenous peoples of the Americas to protect and foster Native cultures throughout the Western Hemisphere. The museum's publishing program seeks to augment awareness of Native American beliefs and lifeways, and to educate the public about the history and significance of Native cultures.

The museum's George Gustav Heye Center in Manhattan opened in 1994; its Cultural Resources Center opened in Suitland, Maryland, in 1998; in 2004, the museum celebrated the grand opening of its primary facility on the National Mall in Washington, D.C.

PHOTOGRAPHY CREDITS
Edward S. Curtis: p. 29 right and p. 30 bottom right; Carmelo Guadagno: p. 30 top left; David Heald: p. 28 left and p. 30 bottom; John K. Hillers: p. 31 top and bottom left; Emry Kopta: p. 31 top right; Charles M. Wood: p. 30 right.

First edition
10 9 8 7 6 5 4 3

Library of Congress Cataloging-in-Publication Data
Dawavendewa, Gerald.
    The Butterfly Dance/story and illustrations by Gerald Dawavendewa.
        p. cm—(Tales of the people)
Summary: Because she is now twelve, Sihumana gets to join the other Hopi in performing the Butterfly Dance, helping to celebrate family and bring gentle rains for the flowers and plants.
    ISBN 978-0-7892-0161-4
    1. Hopi Indians—Juvenile fiction. [1. Hopi Indians—Fiction. 2. Indians of North America—Arizona—Fiction. 3. Rain dances—Fiction. 4. Indian dance—Fiction. 5. Dance—Fiction.] I. Title. II. Series.
PZ7.D32165Bu2000
[E]—dc21   99-045051

For bulk and premium sales and for text adoption procedures, write to Customer Service Manager, Abbeville Press, 137 Varick Street, New York, NY 10013, or call 1-800-ARTBOOK

Visit Abbeville Press online at www.abbeville.com.

About the Author and Illustrator

Gerald Dawavendewa is Hopi–Cherokee, enrolled in the Hopi Tribe and a member of the Sun Clan. He received a B.A. in fine arts from the University of Arizona, where he currently works as a graphic designer with the Lunar and Planetary Laboratory and teaches Native-related courses for the Extended University program and the Center for English as a Second Language. Mr. Dawavendewa, who completed an internship at the National Museum of the American Indian in 1995, has worked as an exhibit specialist, designer, and consultant on American Indian concerns at the Arizona State Museum and at museums and institutions around the country. One of his original artworks, now on display at the University of Arizona, traveled aboard the space shuttle *Endeavour* in 1994.

Tales of the People

Created with the Smithsonian's National Museum of the American Indian (NMAI), **Tales of the People** is a series of children's books celebrating Native American culture with illustrations and stories by Indian artists and writers. In addition to the tales themselves, each book also offers four pages filled with information and photographs exploring various aspects of Native culture, including a glossary of words in different Indian languages.